little Miss Fun

by Roger Hargreaves

Little Miss Fun is as happy
as a lark.

Except when she is organising a party.

And then...

She is even happier than a lark.

Little Miss Fun simply adores parties.

And she likes to invite lots and lots
of people to her parties.

The other Sunday, there were a lot of people making their way to Little Miss Fun's house.

Mr Funny was making funny faces.
Mr Lazy was yawning.
Mr Clumsy was falling over.

And Mr Tall was walking in very small steps . . . so he would not arrive too early!

Mr Forgetful was not with them.
He was at home. Reading a book.
He'd forgotten all about Little Miss Fun's party!

"Never mind,"
laughed Little Miss Fun.
"We can start the party without him!"

She put a record on the record-player.

The record went round and round,
and the music played.

Little Miss Fun asked
Mr Clumsy to dance with her.

And he accepted.

Unfortunately, he stood on her right foot.

"Never mind," she laughed.

Then she ran off to ask Mr Lazy to dance.

Unfortunately, when he put his head on her shoulder, he fell asleep.

And almost flattened her!

"Never mind!" she laughed.

In less than an hour,
Little Miss Fun had made everybody dance:

...the Rumba and the Samba,

...the Rock-and-Roll and the Twist,

...the Charleston and the Cha-Cha-Cha.

Then she led everybody out into the garden.

And they danced all around the house.

All the flowers in the garden were trampled.

"Never mind!"
said Little Miss Fun.
"Let's go back indoors."

"Let's play Simon Says..."
she cried.

"Simon Says...put your feet in the air!"

There was a loud CRASH!

As Mr Tall's foot smashed through the
window pane and shattered it!

"Never mind,"
laughed Little Miss Fun.

And she jumped onto the table
so she could pretend to be a clown
and make her friends laugh.

But nobody laughed.

No wonder!

Everybody was exhausted.

They had all fallen asleep.

"Never mind!" laughed
Little Miss Fun.

And she carried on pretending to be a clown.

Who was she doing it for,
now that everybody was asleep?

Well, she was doing it for a little bird
who had flown in through the broken window.

But there's someone else she is doing it for,
isn't there?

Why, for you, of course!

because you aren't asleep yet...

...but you will be soon.

Fantastic offers for Little Miss fans!

Collect all your Mr. Men or Little Miss books in these superb durable collectors' cases!

Only £5.99 inc. postage and packing, these wipe-clean, hard-wearing cases will give all your Mr. Men or Little Miss books a beautiful new home!

Keep track of your collection with this giant-sized double-sided Mr. Men and Little Miss Collectors' poster.

Collect 6 tokens and we will send you a brilliant giant-sized double-sided collectors' poster! Simply tape a £1 coin to cover postage and packaging in the space provided and fill out the form overleaf.

STICK £1 COIN HERE
(for poster only)

cut along the dotted line and return this whole page

Only need a few Little Miss or Mr. Men to complete your set? You can order any of the titles on the back of the books from our Mr. Men order line on 0870 787 1724. Orders should be delivered between 5 and 7 working days.

TO BE COMPLETED BY AN ADULT

To apply for any of these great offers, ask an adult to complete the details below and send this whole page with the appropriate payment and tokens, to: MR. MEN CLASSIC OFFER, PO BOX 715, HORSHAM RH12 5WG

☐ Please send me a giant-sized double-sided collectors' poster.

AND ☐ I enclose 6 tokens and have taped a £1 coin to the other side of this page.

☐ Please send me ☐ Mr. Men Library case(s) and/or ☐ Little Miss library case(s) at £5.99 each inc P&P

☐ I enclose a cheque/postal order payable to Egmont UK Limited for £.................

OR ☐ Please debit my MasterCard / Visa / Maestro / Delta account (delete as appropriate) for £.................

Card no. ☐☐☐☐☐☐☐☐☐☐☐☐☐☐☐☐☐☐☐☐☐   Security code ☐☐☐

Issue no. (if available) ☐   Start Date ☐☐/☐☐/☐☐   Expiry Date ☐☐/☐☐/☐☐

Fan's name: ....   Date of birth: ....

Address: ....

....

....   Postcode: ....

Name of parent / guardian: ....

Email for parent / guardian: ....

Signature of parent / guardian: ....

Please allow 28 days for delivery. Offer is only available while stocks last. We reserve the right to change the terms of this offer at any time and we offer a 14 day money back guarantee. This does not affect your statutory rights. Offers apply to UK only.

☐ We may occasionally wish to send you information about other Egmont children's books. If you would rather we didn't, please tick this box.

Ref: LIM 001

cut along the dotted line and return this whole page